WACO-McLENNAN COUNTY LIBRARY
1717 AUSTIN AVE
WACO TX 76701

INSIDE MLS

NEW ENGLAND REVOLUTION

BY ANTHONY K. HEWSON

SportsZone
An Imprint of Abdo Publishing
abdobooks.com

abdobooks.com

Published by Abdo Publishing, a division of ABDO, PO Box 398166, Minneapolis, Minnesota 55439. Copyright © 2022 by Abdo Consulting Group, Inc. International copyrights reserved in all countries. No part of this book may be reproduced in any form without written permission from the publisher. SportsZone™ is a trademark and logo of Abdo Publishing.

Printed in the United States of America, North Mankato, Minnesota
052021
092021

Cover Photo: Anthony Nesmith/Cal Sport Media/AP Images
Interior Photos: Robert E. Klein/AP Images, 4–5, 9; Charles Krupa/AP Images, 6; Andy Mead/Icon SMI/Newscom, 10–11; Brad Smith/Icon SMI/Newscom, 13; Otto Greule Jr./Allsport/Getty Images Sport/Getty Images 15; David Carson/AP Images, 16; Wade Jackson/Icon SMI/Newscom, 19, 37; Bill Kostroun/AP Images, 20; John Jones/Icon Sportswire/AP Images, 23; Lee K. Marriner UPI Photo Service/Newscom, 24–25; Scott Bales/Icon SMI/Newscom, 26; Bret Hartman/AP Images, 29; Fred Kfoury III/Icon Sportswire/AP Images, 30, 34; Elise Amendola/AP Images, 33; Matt Slocum/AP Images, 38; Pablo Martinez Monsivais/AP Images, 41; Steven Senne/AP Images, 42

Editor: Patrick Donnelly
Series Designer: Dan Peluso

Library of Congress Control Number: 2020948187

Publisher's Cataloging-in-Publication Data

Names: Hewson, Anthony K., author.
Title: New England Revolution / by Anthony K. Hewson
Description: Minneapolis, Minnesota : Abdo Publishing, 2022 | Series: Inside MLS | Includes online resources and index.
Identifiers: ISBN 9781532194788 (lib. bdg.) | ISBN 9781098214449 (ebook)
Subjects: LCSH: New England Revolution (Soccer team)--Juvenile literature. | Soccer teams--Juvenile literature. | Professional sports franchises--Juvenile literature. | Sports Teams--Juvenile literature.
Classification: DDC 796.334--dc23

TABLE OF CONTENTS

CHAPTER 1
A NEW NEW ENGLAND 4

CHAPTER 2
A SOCCER REVOLUTION 14

CHAPTER 3
THE MAIN MINUTEMEN 24

CHAPTER 4
REVOLUTIONARY MOMENTS 34

TIMELINE	44
TEAM FACTS	45
GLOSSARY	46
MORE INFORMATION	47
ONLINE RESOURCES	47
INDEX	48
ABOUT THE AUTHOR	48

CHAPTER 1

A NEW NEW ENGLAND

As the New England Revolution walked out of the home locker room and onto the Gillette Stadium turf on October 12, 2002, the task was clear. In the third meeting of their Major League Soccer (MLS) playoff series with the Columbus Crew, all the Revs needed was a point.

In the first two matches, New England had a draw and a victory. Columbus had to win Game 3 to even the series and force a tiebreaker. The winner would advance to the MLS Cup.

New England had played in MLS since the league's first season in 1996. But the team had little to show for it. The Revs had made the playoffs twice in the first six years but failed to advance. Things had changed by 2002, however.

Revolution defender Carlos Llamosa (18) battles with Columbus's Dante Washington in their 2002 playoff game.

Taylor Twellman celebrates his second goal against the Chicago Fire in the 2002 playoffs.

The team had a new coach in former English Premier League star Steve Nicol. It had exciting new players including striker Taylor Twellman and midfielder Steve Ralston. And Gillette Stadium was brand new.

Twellman led the league in combined goals and assists that season. The new-and-improved Revs made the playoffs, though just barely. They closed the season on a 5–0–1 run to sneak into first place in the Eastern Conference. But they had a losing record overall for the year, and a deep playoff run seemed unlikely.

STAYING HOT

Instead, the team's run of late-season success continued into the playoffs. Twellman scored a game-winning goal and added another tally as the Revs beat the Chicago Fire in the conference semifinals. That sent New England to the conference finals against Columbus. The Crew was an original MLS team like New England. But Columbus had been much more successful thus far.

The series opened with a scoreless tie on October 6 at Gillette Stadium. The series then shifted to Columbus. Almost immediately, New England grabbed the lead. Defender Jay Heaps, rarely a goal scorer, found the net off a corner kick in the third minute. New England then held on for 87 minutes to get its first road playoff win.

That left the Revs on the verge of something big in Game 3. The team's defense was feeling pretty good about itself. It had surrendered only two goals all playoffs and none yet against Columbus. So when goals by Ralston and Wolde Harris fired New England to a 2–0 halftime lead, it looked like that would be more than enough.

HANGING ON

After 80 minutes, Columbus suddenly figured out how to attack. The Crew scored two quick goals, tying the match in the 85th minute. From there, neither team was able to score the winner, so the match went to a 10-minute extra time period. If Columbus won, it would tie the series and force another extra time period in which the first goal would win the series.

New England's defense may have gotten lost for those five minutes late in the game. But the team still had confidence. All it had to do was not allow another goal for 10 minutes. And that was exactly what the Revs did. New England advanced to the league playoff final.

New England's Steve Ralston, *right*, battles for the ball against the Crew's Eric Denton.

Making the MLS Cup was a historic moment for the Revs. And there was a special bonus that came with playing in that year's final. It was at Gillette Stadium, where the Revs would enjoy a home-field advantage. Their fans had been waiting six years for a moment like that.

A huge crowd showed up to watch the Revolution host the Galaxy in the 2002 MLS Cup.

More than 61,000 fans packed in to watch their Revs face the mighty LA Galaxy. Unlike New England, the Galaxy had been one of the best teams in MLS since 1996. They had more scoring chances throughout the match. But the Revs' defense

A GOAL AND AN EJECTION

Jay Heaps was the hero in Game 2 of New England's conference final with Columbus. But the defender nearly cost his team dearly. Heaps scored in the third minute but was ejected in the 39th. That meant his team had to play with only 10 men for the rest of the match. And Heaps had to miss the crucial third game of the series.

was able to hang on, not allowing a single goal. And the Galaxy defense shut down Taylor Twellman and Steve Ralston.

After 90 scoreless minutes, the game went to a sudden-death extra time period. The first goal would win. In the 113th minute, Carlos Ruiz buried the winner for Los Angeles. It was the first title for the Galaxy and a heartbreaking defeat for New England. But the Revolution would be back.

Twellman, *left*, dribbles away from a Galaxy defender during the 2002 MLS Cup.

CHAPTER 2

A SOCCER REVOLUTION

The Boston area is home to some of the most passionate sports fans in the United States. They love their teams such as baseball's Red Sox and football's New England Patriots. MLS wanted to get in on that. The league awarded the Boston area one of its original franchises in 1996. Now the question was whether local fans would embrace soccer like they did the other sports.

New England certainly had a long history with the game. The Oneida Football Club was the first organized team in the United States. The club played a game similar to soccer in the 1860s. A team out of Fall River, Massachusetts, called the Marksmen was one of the first great teams in the country. The club, nicknamed the "American Menace," won the

Defender Alexi Lalas was one of the Revolution's early stars.

Alberto Naveda celebrates his goal against the New York/New Jersey MetroStars.

National Challenge Cup five times between 1917 and 1931. That competition continues today as the US Open Cup. It's open to men's soccer teams from all levels in the United States.

Like the other nine original MLS clubs, New England's new team played at an American football stadium. It shared the home of the Patriots in Foxborough, Massachusetts. It also shared the regional name "New England" instead of a city or state. And it featured a similarly patriotic nickname.

In a contest to name the team, a high school student suggested "Revolution." Massachusetts played a key role in the American Revolution. The team's colors matched the US flag's red, white, and blue.

Those were particularly familiar colors for a few key members of the 1996 Revolution. Alexi Lalas and Joe-Max Moore were regulars on the US men's national team. Both would play leading roles with their new club.

GETTING STARTED

The Revs played their first-ever match on the road against the Tampa Bay Mutiny on April 13, 1996. Rob Ukrop scored the first goal in team history in the 20th minute. But the Mutiny took the lead five minutes later and the Revs lost 3–2.

The club got its first victory the next week, but it did so without any of its players scoring. A last-minute own goal by the New York/New Jersey MetroStars was the only scoring in the match. New England headed home with a 1–1–0 record. And the Revs then started their first winning streak by beating DC United in their first home game.

ANOTHER BOSTON–NEW YORK RIVALRY

The Red Sox and the Yankees. The Patriots and the Jets. The Bruins and the Rangers. The Celtics and the Knicks. Boston and New York teams have long histories of not liking each other. Their soccer clubs are no exception. The Revs and the New York Red Bulls are both original MLS teams. Their first meeting was New England's first-ever win on April 20, 1996. The Revs have historically fared better in the rivalry, especially at Gillette Stadium. They didn't lose a home regular-season match to their New York opponents from 2002 to 2013.

But there was not much more to celebrate for the 1996 Revs. The club finished in last place, one of just two teams in the league to miss the playoffs. Both the Revs and MLS struggled to find their footing in the early years. Attendance was low and the quality of play had a reputation for being poor.

New England made the playoffs in 1997 and in 2000 but failed to advance each time. But things had turned around by the early 2000s. Strikers Taylor Twellman and Pat Noonan and midfielder Steve Ralston led a strong scoring attack. Shalrie Joseph was rock-solid in defense. And keeper Matt Reis manned the net. They formed a solid core for years to come. The magical run to the 2002 MLS Cup showed New England could be a soccer hotbed. A crowd of 61,316 fans packed into brand-new Gillette Stadium to see their team play for a title.

Taylor Twellman, *right*, breaks away in the 2005 MLS Cup.

The Revs were finally a winning team. They made the playoffs in each of the next seven seasons. That included three consecutive trips to the MLS Cup from 2005 to 2007. But they became known for some painful losses. The Revs lost the 2002 and 2005 finals 1–0 in extra time. They lost in 2006 in a penalty kick shootout. And in 2007, it was a 2–1 loss.

US national team star Jermaine Jones helped the red-hot Revolution reach the 2014 MLS Cup.

The Revs did win one trophy in this time span—the 2007 US Open Cup. After a thrilling overtime win against the minor league Carolina RailHawks in the semifinals, New England beat FC Dallas in the final 3–2.

But that was the last big win for the team's core of players. Twellman and Ralston both retired after the 2009 season. Coach Steve Nicol was fired in 2011. In 2012 the club missed the playoffs for the third season in a row, the longest streak in team history.

MOVING FORWARD

Former Revs player Jay Heaps replaced Nicol at head coach. By 2013 he had them back in the playoffs. In 2014 New England recaptured some magic like it had in 2002. The team signed US national team midfielder Jermaine Jones in August. With Jones in the lineup, the Revs went 8–1–1 and finished second in their conference.

The hot streak continued in the playoffs. New England didn't lose a game as it returned to the MLS Cup. But the result was yet another bitter defeat. New England again lost to the Galaxy in extra time.

Revs fans hoped it was the start of another golden era. Instead, Heaps was fired in 2017 after the Revs missed the playoffs in back-to-back seasons. The next head coach, former national team goalkeeper Brad Friedel, didn't fare much better. He was fired after winning two of 12 games to open the 2019 season.

New England soccer was at a crossroads. Not only were the Revs failing on the field, they were being outclassed by newer teams. The Revs were an original MLS club but were no longer one of the league's premier teams.

Other newer teams had built new soccer-specific stadiums. The Revs still played in the home of the Patriots, which was too big to allow for an intimate soccer setting. The Revs' supporters' group on matchday numbered only a few hundred people. Some fans accused the team's owners, who also owned the Patriots, of ignoring their soccer team.

But the Revs hired an MLS and US soccer legend as their new coach. Bruce Arena had won five MLS Cups in his career. He won more games with the US men's national team than anyone else. He had the résumé to bring New England back to relevancy.

Arena helped rescue the 2019 team. After their 2–8–2 start, the Revs went on an 11-match unbeaten streak. That was the longest in club history. Not only were they winning, the team was having fun. Even though they lost in the first round, making it back to the playoffs was a big accomplishment. Then, one year later, promising young stars Carles Gil and Gustavo Bou led the Revs back to the conference title game. Once again the future looked bright in New England.

Gustavo Bou and the Revolution bounced back with a strong season in 2019.

CHAPTER 3

THE MAIN
MINUTEMEN

When MLS began in 1996, it designed a process to make sure each team had some star players. That was how the Revs ended up with US national team players Alexi Lalas, Mike Burns, and Joe-Max Moore. Lalas struggled at times to replicate his play with the national team, and Burns was injured for half of 1996. But Moore was outstanding.

The forward scored 11 goals in his first 13 appearances in New England. He went on to become the team's first all-time leading scorer. Moore's scoring ability earned him a contract to play for Everton of the English Premier League in 1999. But he came back in 2003 to finish his career with the Revs. Injuries limited his scoring totals, but he retired with 41 goals in 96 games for New England.

Joe-Max Moore, left, scored seven goals and had 15 assists during the 1998 season.

Taylor Twellman, *left*, and Steve Ralston made for a lethal combo.

Moore's second stint in New England overlapped with that of another star forward. Taylor Twellman went on to surpass Moore as the No. 1 scorer in Revs history. He also made his case as the greatest overall player in team history.

Twellman was a star immediately upon joining the Revolution in 2002. He scored the game-winning goal in his first start and led New England to the MLS Cup. Twellman's career peaked in 2005 when he won the league's Most Valuable Player (MVP) Award. In 174 games, Twellman scored 101 goals. The only thing that could stop him was injuries. Concussions limited him to 16 games in 2008 and just two in 2009. He retired from pro soccer in 2010 and later became a broadcaster.

Future US national team captain Clint Dempsey also got his start in New England. The striker was the Revolution's first-round pick in the 2004 draft and scored 25 goals in 71 matches. After the 2006 season his contract was transferred to Fulham of England's Premier League for $4 million. That was a record transfer fee for an MLS player at the time.

SMOOTH SETUP MAN

If Twellman and Dempsey were scoring the goals, Steve Ralston was probably the one setting them up. Ralston was the club's top midfielder from 2002 to 2010. He was already a star when he came to New England. He was the first MLS Rookie of the Year in 1996 with the Tampa Bay Mutiny.

Ralston reached even greater heights in New England. He helped the club reach four MLS Cups. He set the Revs record for career assists with 73 and retired with the most in MLS history. He also won the league's Fair Play award three times, showing his professionalism. Ralston was often a Revs captain until his retirement in 2010.

Shalrie Joseph was the Revs' iron man. Joseph was a constant presence in the New England midfield from 2003 to 2012. Joseph wound up as the team leader in games (261) and minutes played (22,866). Joseph not only played a lot, he played very well. He was named one of MLS' Best XI players four times.

MODERN REVS

At 16, Diego Fagundez was the youngest player in Revs history when he made his debut in 2011.

STEVE NICOL

Four coaches in six years could not make New England a winner until Steve Nicol arrived in 2002. Nicol coached the Revs to eight straight playoff appearances, a streak that included four MLS Cups. It was an unprecedented run of success for a club that had struggled. He also won the first trophy for the club, the 2007 US Open Cup. The team had declined by 2011 and Nicol was fired. But he remains by far the club leader in wins and games managed.

Shalrie Joseph was a force in the Revolution midfield for a decade.

Defender Andrew Farrell has proven to be a reliable presence in the Revolution defense.

Fagundez became the youngest to score a goal that August. He then went on to rocket up the team and MLS leaderboards. In ten seasons with New England, Fagundez scored 53 goals and added 45 assists in more than 250 games.

Players don't get much more home grown than defender Chris Tierney. Born and raised in the Boston area, Tierney was New England's first-round pick in the 2008 supplemental draft. He then went on to an 11-year career with the Revs. Tierney mostly played left back but he could do a lot more than that.

Tierney played all across the back line and at midfielder. He even had a scoring touch. He and Twellman are the only two Revolution players to score in an MLS Cup. Tierney retired from pro soccer in 2018. He then joined the Revs' front office.

Joseph, Fagundez, and Tierney were all known for their reliability and durability. Defender Andrew Farrell is no different. Farrell entered MLS in 2013. Over the next eight seasons, he led all non-goalkeepers in minutes played. It helps he can play all over the back line. Farrell has played left, right, and center back. And he played those positions well, earning the Revs' Defender of the Year award in 2015, 2018, and 2019.

GUARDIAN OF THE GOAL

Between the posts, one Revs man stands out above the rest. Matt Reis holds almost every New England goalkeeping record there is, including games played, wins, saves, and shutouts. Reis had already been in MLS for five years when he came to New England in 2003. He played 11 more seasons and was a four-time finalist for Goalkeeper of the Year.

Reis was also known for his work off the field. He raised money for numerous charities and was often the team's nominee for MLS Humanitarian of the Year, an award he won in 2013. Reis was attending that year's Boston Marathon when two bombs exploded at the finish line. His father-in-law was injured in the blast. Reis was able to stop his bleeding long enough to save his life.

In 2020 the Revs celebrated their 25th anniversary season. They named an all-time team based on the vote of the fans. Reis was the goalkeeper. The defenders were Farrell, Tierney, and former US national teamer Michael Parkhurst. In midfield was national team co-leading scorer Dempsey, Lee Nguyen, Fagundez, Joseph, and Ralston. Up top were legendary forwards Moore and Twellman.

Goalkeeper Matt Reis started 253 regular-season games over 11 seasons in New England.

CHAPTER 4

REVOLUTIONARY MOMENTS

A crowd of 32,864 fans was waiting at Foxboro Stadium on April 27, 1996. It was the first home game in New England Revolution history. And the opponent was DC United, who would go on to be that season's MLS champion.

The attendance was bigger than the crowd for that day's Red Sox game. The club's first supporters' group, the Midnight Riders, stood and cheered all game long behind the south goal. Win or lose, the fans were in a mood to celebrate.

They roared when their club scored a tying goal in the 78th minute. In those days of MLS, tie games were decided by a penalty kick shootout. Darren Sawatzky scored the match-winner to send the new fans home happy.

The Midnight Riders supporters' group has been with the Revolution from the start.

GOLDEN ERA

The fans had to be patient before tasting extended success. But it was worth the wait. The Revs' thrilling 2002 playoff run earned them the right to play for a championship. They fell just short, losing a heartbreaker to the LA Galaxy. But the best was yet to come.

RECORD ATTENDANCE

The 2002 MLS Cup final drew 61,316 fans to Gillette Stadium. That set an attendance record for the MLS championship. No game came even close to matching it until 2018. Atlanta United set many MLS attendance records that season, including drawing 73,019 fans to its home MLS Cup.

The 2005 New England team was a special one. Taylor Twellman was named the league MVP. He joined Shalrie Joseph and Clint Dempsey on the MLS Best XI team. The Revs finished first in their conference and made it back to the MLS Cup. It was a rematch with the Galaxy.

The match played out almost the exact same way as 2002. It again went to extra time 0–0. And again, LA scored. This time little-used midfielder Guillermo Ramirez played hero. But unlike 2002, extra time did not end after the first goal. New England had several good scoring chances. But time ran out, and LA got the victory again.

Clint Dempsey establishes control of the ball during the 2005 MLS Cup against the LA Galaxy.

Revs defender Jay Heaps covers his face after his penalty kick was saved in the 2006 MLS Cup.

The Revs came even closer in 2006. Against the Houston Dynamo, they again failed to score through 90 minutes. That was 270 minutes plus extra time that New England couldn't score in championship action. But Houston didn't score either, so the game went to extra time.

Fittingly, Twellman was the man to snap the Revs' scoring drought. In the 113th minute, he received a pass in the 18-yard box, took a single touch, and fired a shot. After 346 minutes,

New England finally had a goal in the MLS Cup—one that was poised to win the team its first trophy.

The joy did not last long. Houston's Brian Ching scored 71 seconds later. Neither team could score for the rest of extra time, so the match went to penalty kicks.

New England converted its first two. One of those even came from keeper Matt Reis. Reis later used his hands to stop Brad Davis. In the fifth round of shots, Ching scored to put Houston ahead by one. It was up to defender Jay Heaps to keep the Revs alive. Heaps tried to fool the Houston keeper, but his shot ended up weakly rolling toward the goal. It was an easy save, and New England suffered another tough loss.

As the 2007 Revs were making another MLS Cup run, they were also pursuing another trophy. They were having their best year yet in the US Open Cup. New England faced a clear path to the final, drawing three minor-league teams. But it turned out not to be easy at all. The Revs scored a one-goal victory over the Harrisburg City Islanders, who played two levels below MLS. Then in the semifinal, they needed extra time to beat the Carolina RailHawks, a club from one level below.

The Revs faced FC Dallas of MLS in the final. The match was at Dallas' home field. New England built a 3–1 lead but had to hang on after Dallas scored a second goal in the 64th minute. It was the first trophy for the Revolution.

Just over a month later, New England was back in the MLS Cup. One of these years, New England had to break through. That was the hope of the Revs supporters, at least. Many of them traveled to Washington, DC, in 2007 to see their team try again. Many more were back at Gillette Stadium watching on video.

New England had another rematch, this time with the Dynamo. And for the first time in an MLS Cup, New England managed to score before extra time. Twellman headed home a Ralston pass in the 20th minute. The Revs defense was playing well, and they took their 1–0 lead into halftime.

But Houston changed formations in the second half. The Dynamo started to get more scoring chances. They tied the match in the 61st minute. With the Revs defense reeling, Houston then took the lead in the 74th. New England had a few more scoring chances but could not convert.

The Revs got a bit of revenge on Houston in 2008. But it wasn't in the MLS Cup. As the winners of the US Open Cup, New England qualified for the North American SuperLiga.

Taylor Twellman, *right*, celebrates after scoring against the Dynamo in the 2007 MLS Cup.

That tournament matched up the top teams from Mexico and the United States. Houston made it as MLS Cup champions.

New England won its group and defeated three Mexican teams on the way to the final. It was a rematch with Houston, but the game was in New England. Houston scored in extra

Carles Gil, *right*, celebrates one of his 10 goals during the 2019 season.

time to take a 2–1 lead, but this time New England struck back. Shalrie Joseph scored in the 102nd minute and the match went to a shootout. This time, it was the Revs that came out on top.

ANOTHER RUN OF SUCCESS

It seemed like the Revs were primed for several more Cup runs. But they had to wait seven years for another one. Twellman and Ralston were long gone. But the team had a new core of players with defender Andrew Farrell and midfielder Lee Nguyen.

New England made it back to the MLS Cup in 2014. Its opponent was an old friend, the LA Galaxy. They hosted the match in Carson, California. Chris Tierney scored for the Revs in the 79th minute, and the match entered extra time tied 1–1. Yet again, the Revs were doomed by an extra time goal. Robbie Keane scored for LA in the 111th minute, and New England couldn't respond. The Revs became the first team to lose five MLS Cups.

It took six years until New England won another playoff game. The 2020 Revs were just so-so in the regular season. But they were able to knock off Montreal in the first round. Carles Gil, the 2019 MLS Newcomer of the Year, and Gustavo Bou scored the goals.

Next up was Philadelphia, the league's top team during the regular season. Led by a strong performance from Gil, the Revs shut them out 2–0. Bou then scored two goals and Gil added another in a 3–1 win over Orlando. New England was just one win away from another MLS Cup. But the team's run came to an end in a heartbreaking 1–0 loss to the Columbus Crew.

Nonetheless with a young core in Bou and Gil, veteran leaders like Farrell, and an experienced manager in Bruce Arena, Revs fans hoped a championship was just around the corner.

TIMELINE

1996 — The New England Revolution plays its first match in team history on April 13, a 3–2 loss in Tampa to the Mutiny.

1996 — The Revs win their first game, a 1–0 shutout of the New York/New Jersey MetroStars on April 20.

2002 — New England plays in its first MLS Cup final, losing in extra time to the LA Galaxy 1–0 on October 20.

2005 — New England gets an MLS Cup rematch with the Galaxy on November 13 but drops another 1–0 match in extra time.

2006 — Taylor Twellman scores the first Revs goal in an MLS Cup, but New England falls in a penalty shootout to the Houston Dynamo on November 12.

2007 — New England wins its first trophy, beating FC Dallas 3–2 on October 3 in the US Open Cup final.

2007 — The Revolution lose a 1–0 halftime lead in the MLS Cup, falling 2–1 to the Dynamo on November 18.

2008 — New England beats Houston in a penalty shootout on August 5 to win the 2008 North American SuperLiga.

2014 — New England loses in the MLS Cup to the Galaxy for the third time, a 2–1 loss after extra time on December 7.

2020 — The Revs win their first playoff game since 2014 and then advance all the way to the conference finals.

TEAM FACTS

FIRST SEASON
1996

STADIUM
Foxboro Stadium (1996–01)
Gillette Stadium (2002–)

US OPEN CUP TITLES
2007

KEY PLAYERS
Gustavo Bou (2019–)
Clint Dempsey (2004–06)
Diego Fagundez (2011–20)
Andrew Farrell (2013–)
Carles Gil (2019–)
Shalrie Joseph (2003–12, 2014)
Joe-Max Moore (1996–99, 2003–04)
Lee Nguyen (2012–17)
Michael Parkhurst (2005–08)
Steve Ralston (2002–09)
Matt Reis (2003–13)
Chris Tierney (2008–18)
Taylor Twellman (2002–09)

KEY COACHES
Bruce Arena (2019–)
Steve Nicol (2002–11)

LANDON DONOVAN MVP AWARD
Taylor Twellman (2005)

MLS GOLDEN BOOT
Pat Noonan (2004)
Taylor Twellman (2002, 2005),

SIGI SCHMID COACH OF THE YEAR AWARD
Steve Nicol (2002)

MLS DEFENDER OF THE YEAR
Jose Goncalves (2013)
Michael Parkhurst (2007)

MLS NEWCOMER OF THE YEAR
Carles Gil (2019)

MLS ROOKIE OF THE YEAR
Clint Dempsey (2004)
Michael Parkhurst (2005)

GLOSSARY

assists
Passes that lead directly to goals.

conference
A group of teams within a league.

extra time
Two 15-minute periods added to a game if the score is tied at the end of regulation.

midfielder
A player who stays mostly in the middle third of the field and links the defenders with the forwards.

own goal
A goal that is last touched by a member of the defense.

penalty shootout
A tiebreaking shootout of alternating kicks from the penalty spot that decides who wins the game.

retired
Ended one's career.

rivalry
A fierce and ongoing competition between two players or teams.

rookie
A first-year player.

shutouts
Games in which one team does not score.

striker
A forward whose main job is to score goals.

veterans
Players who have played many years.

MORE INFORMATION

BOOKS

Kortemeier, Todd. *Total Soccer*. Minneapolis, MN: Abdo Publishing, 2017.

Marthaler, Jon. *Ultimate Soccer Road Trip*. Minneapolis, MN: Abdo Publishing, 2019.

Trusdell, Brian. *Soccer Record Breakers*. Minneapolis, MN: Abdo Publishing, 2016.

ONLINE RESOURCES

To learn more about the New England Revolution, please visit **abdobooklinks.com** or scan this QR code. These links are routinely monitored and updated to provide the most current information available.

INDEX

Arena, Bruce, 22, 43

Bou, Gustavo, 22, 43
Burns, Mike, 24

Ching, Brian, 39

Davis, Brad, 39
Dempsey, Clint, 27, 32, 36

Fagundez, Diego, 28, 31, 32, 43
Farrell, Andrew, 31, 32, 42, 43
Friedel, Brad, 21

Gil, Carles, 22, 43

Harris, Wolde, 8
Heaps, Jay, 7, 12, 21, 39
Jones, Jermaine, 21
Joseph, Shalrie, 18, 28, 31, 32, 36, 42

Keane, Robbie, 43

Lalas, Alexi, 17, 24

Moore, Joe-Max, 17, 24, 27, 32

Nguyen, Lee, 32, 42
Nicol, Steve, 7, 21, 28
Noonan, Pat, 18

Parkhurst, Michael, 32

Ralston, Steve, 7–8, 12, 21, 27–28, 32, 40, 42, 43
Ramirez, Guillermo, 36
Reis, Matt, 18, 32, 39
Ruiz, Carlos, 12

Sawatzky, Darren, 34

Tierney, Chris, 31, 32, 43
Twellman, Taylor, 7, 12, 18, 21, 27, 31, 32, 36, 38, 40, 42, 43

Ukrop, Rob, 17

ABOUT THE AUTHOR

Anthony K. Hewson has followed American soccer since before the MLS days. Originally from San Diego, he now lives in the Bay Area with his wife and dogs.